WHAT DOES WORD BIRD SEE?

by Jane Belk Moncure
illustrated by Vera Gohman

THE CHILD'S WORLD
MANKATO, MN 56001

Library of Congress Cataloging in Publication Data

Moncure, Jane Belk.
What does Word Bird see?

(Word Birds for early birds)
Summary: Word Bird sees the homes of a number of different animals. Includes vocabulary list.
1. Animals—Habitations—Fiction.
2. Vocabulary] I. Gohman, Vera Kennedy, 1922- ill. II. Title. III. Series: Moncure, Jane Belk. Word Birds for early birds.
PZ7.M739Whb [E] 81-21594
ISBN 0-89565-220-X -1991 Edition AACR2

WHAT DOES WORD BIRD SEE?

Word Bird sees

a hole
in the
tree.

Who lives there?

Squirrels.

"Hi, squirrels."

Word Bird sees

a hole
in the
grass.

Who lives there?

Rabbits.

"Hi, rabbits."

Word Bird sees

a hole
in the
house.

Who lives there?

A mouse.

"Hi, mouse."

Word Bird sees

a house made of sticks.

Who lives there?

A beaver.

"Hi, beaver."

Word Bird sees

a hole
in a
mound.

Who lives there?

Ants.

"Hi, ants."

Word Bird sees

a
pretty
shell.

Who lives there?

A turtle.

"Hi, turtle."

Word Bird sees

a
funny
shape.

Who lives there?

Bees!

"Bye, bye, bees."

Can you read these words with 

?

hole 

tree 

squirrel 

grass 

rabbit 

mouse 

stick 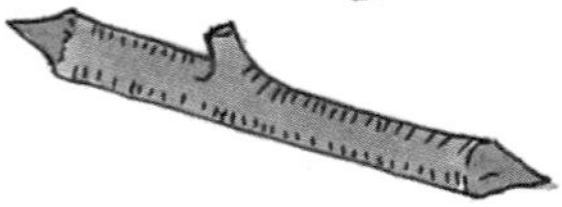

beaver 

mound 

ant 

shell 

turtle 

bee